Fancy NANCY

and the Posh Puppy

Written by
Jane O'Connor

Illustrated by
Robin Preiss Glasser

HarperCollinsPublishers

Fancy Nancy and the Posh Puppy
Text copyright © 2007 by Jane O'Connor
Illustrations copyright © 2007 by Robin Preiss Glasser
Manufactured in China.

For information address HarperCollins Children's Books, a division of HarperCollins Publishers,
195 Broadway, New York, NY 10007.
www.harpercollinschildrens.com

Library of Congress Cataloging-in-Publication Data
O'Connor, Jane.
    Fancy Nancy and the posh puppy / by Jane O'Connor ; pictures by Robin Preiss Glasser. — 1st ed.
       p.   cm.
    Summary: Nancy wants to adopt a special puppy so that she is no longer the only fancy member of her family, but after
a day of puppysitting a papillon, she realizes that being fancy is not always the most important thing.
    ISBN-13: 978-0-06-054213-9 (trade bdg.) — ISBN-10: 0-06-054213-6 (trade bdg.)
    ISBN-13: 978-0-06-054215-3 (lib. bdg.) — ISBN-10: 0-06-054215-2 (lib. bdg.)
    [1. Papillon dog—Fiction. 2. Dogs—Fiction. 3. Individuality—Fiction. 4. Family life—Fiction.] I. Preiss-Glasser, Robin, ill. II. Title.
PZ7.O222Fad 2007   2006030428
[E]—dc22   CIP
                                                                                                            AC

Typography by Jeanne L. Hogle
16 17 SCP 20 19
❖
First Edition

For Margaret Anastas, an absolute firecracker of an editor, all my thanks
for ushering Nancy into the world and making the whole experience so much fun
—J.O'C.

For my agent and friend, Faith Hamlin, who has doggedly helped me
through thick and thin
—R.P.G.

I am ecstatic. (That's a fancy word for happy.)
We're going to get a puppy—a real one.

I hope we get a papillon, like our neighbor's dog.
You say it like this: *pappy-yawn.* In French it means
butterfly.

I help Mrs. DeVine take care of Jewel.

We take her to
the beauty salon.

We buy her new ensembles.
(That's a fancy word for clothes.)

Papillons are so posh.
(That's a fancy word for fancy.)

There is only one problem . . . my parents.
"Papillons like to stay indoors," my dad says.
"They're too little."

I shake my head. Too big. Too brown. Too plain.
Sometimes it's hard being the only fancy person in a family.

Then I get an idea that is spectacular.
(That's a fancy word for great.)
We can puppysit for Jewel!

My parents say okay.
So does Mrs. DeVine.
My family will see how happy we'll
be with a papillon puppy.

I introduce Jewel to my doll, Marabelle.

I show my sister how
to groom Jewel . . .

. . . and how to scoop
her poop.

My sister wants to hold and kiss Jewel.
I tell her, "You must be gentle."
"What a responsible girl you are," my mom says.
"Some dog is going to be very lucky."

"Merci," I say. (That's French for "thank you.")

Two of my friends are walking their dogs.
"Come over to my house," I say. "I'm puppysitting.
All the dogs can play together."

Rusty splashes in the wading pool.
Jewel hides behind my legs.

Scamp plays fetch.

"Go, Jewel. Go get the ball!" I yell.
Jewel just looks at me.

"She gets exhausted pretty quickly,"
I tell my friends. (That's a fancy word
for tired.)

While Jewel gets her beauty
rest, we have refreshments.

Oh, no! Look what my sister is doing.
Poor Jewel is terrified!

"Mom! Come quick. Jewel is going to be sick!"

"When we get our papillon,
I'm not letting her near it," I say.

My mom whispers, "She doesn't know better.
She was trying to be nice."
I know that.

We take Jewel back to her house.
She is a perfect dog for Mrs. DeVine.
But maybe she isn't the perfect dog for us.

I'm so sad I hardly get fancy when we go
to the King's Crown for dinner.

On the way home, we drive by the animal shelter.
"Let's take a look," my mom says. "All those dogs need
a family to love them."

I ask the lady, "Are there any fancy dogs here?"
And she says, "I think I have just the dog for you. She's funny and playful and smart and cuddly. Her name is Frenchy."

Hmmmm . . . Frenchy? I like the sound of that.

Frenchy runs right to me and jumps in my lap.
She likes it when my sister hugs her.

Frenchy is the perfect dog for us.

My dad says Frenchy is a La Salle
spaniel. That is a very unique breed.
(Unique is fancy for one of a kind.)

You know what?
Maybe that's even better than fancy.